I0815047

SIMPLY **SCIENCE**

The Simple Science of MOTION

by Emily James

CAPSTONE PRESS
a capstone imprint

A+ Books are published by Capstone Press,
1710 Roe Crest Drive, North Mankato, Minnesota 56003
www.mycapstone.com

Library of Congress Cataloging-in-Publication Data
Library of Congress Cataloging-in-Publication Data is available on the Library of Congress website.

ISBN: 978-1-5435-1227-4 (library hardover) — 978-1-5435-1229-8 (paperback) — 978-1-5435-1231-1 (ebook)

Summary: Find out what motion is, how it changes, and more

Editorial Credits
Jaclyn Jaycox, editor; Brenton Slingsby and Ashlee Suker, designers; Tracy Cummins, media researcher; Kathy McColley, production specialist

Photo Credits
iStockphoto: DaveAlan, Cover, skodonnell, 16-17; Shutterstock: 2xSamara.com, 23, 29 (red ball), Aphelleon, 24-25, artlula, 15, bdavid32, 6, Blend Images, 18, BlueOrange Studio, 21, Cheryl Casey, 28-29, fotum, 13 Inset, Hurst Photo, 5, HYS_NP, 19, Kitch Bain, Back Cover, 2-3, 30, 32, Kuznetsov Alexey, 9, Maya Kruchankova, 12-13, modina, 20 Inset, Monkey Business Images, 22, Patrick Foto, 14, Phanuwat_Nandee, 20, pirke, Back Cover, 2-3, 30, Saranya Loisamutr, 8, Sergey Novikov, 10-11, Shooter Bob Square Lenses, 21 Inset, Simon Kovacic, 7, Soonthorn Wongsaita, 4 Inset, Standret, 26-27, StudioOneNine, 29 (baseball), supergenijalac, 4

Note to Parents, Teachers, and Librarians

This Simply Science book uses full color photographs and a nonfiction format to introduce the concept of motion. *The Simple Science of Motion* is designed to be read aloud to a pre-reader or to be read independently by an early reader. Photographs help listeners and early readers understand the text and concepts discussed. The book encourages further learning by including the following sections: Table of Contents, Glossary, Read More, Internet Sites, Critical Thinking Questions, and Index. Early readers may need assistance using these features.

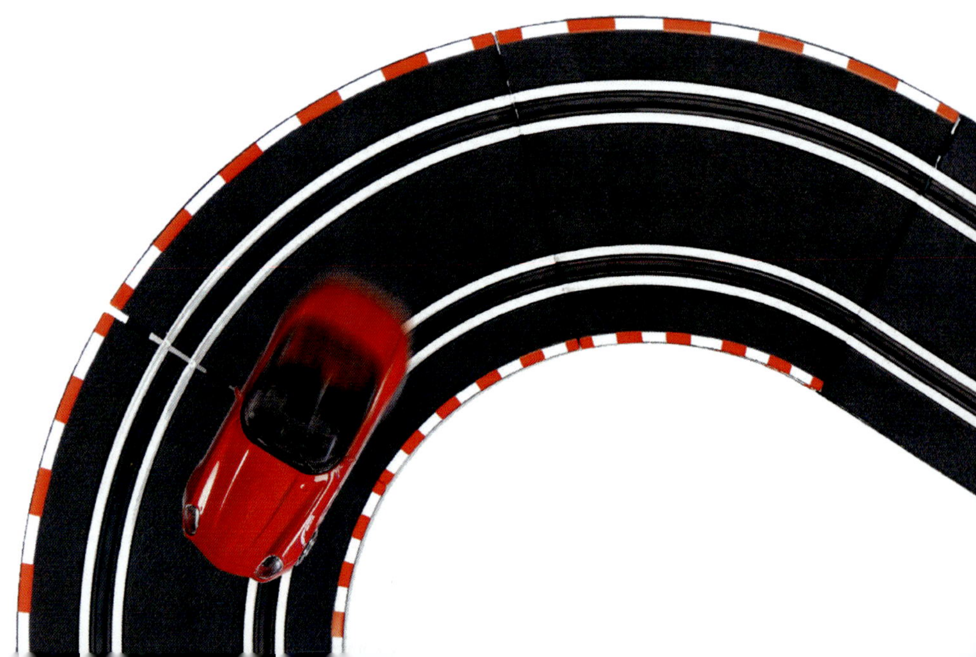

Printed in the United States 5578

Table of CONTENTS

What Is Motion? 4
Fast and Slow 8
Changes in Motion 12
Facts About Friction 18
Gravity 22
Flying Through Space! 24
Motion All Around 26

Testing Friction 28
Glossary 30
Read More 31
Internet Sites 31
Critical Thinking Questions 32
Index 32

What Is Motion?

A car zooms by. Tree branches sway in the breeze. An airplane flies high in the sky. Anything that moves from one place to another is in motion.

There are lots of different words to describe motion. You can run, walk, jump, dance, swim, slide, and skate.

Things can move in different directions. A helicopter can move up and down, forward and backward.

A train can move in straight or curved lines. A merry-go-round can move around and around.

Fast and Slow

Some things move quickly, like a race car or a baseball. Other things move slowly, like a baby crawling or a turtle walking.

How fast something moves is called its speed. You can measure speed. When the needle on a car speedometer points to 60, it means it will take one hour for the car to move 60 miles (97 kilometers).

The strength of a push or pull on an object can make it go faster or slow down more quickly. If you are pushing a shopping cart and start to run, the cart will move faster.

When something increases in speed, it's called acceleration. When you slow down and pull on the cart handle, it slows down quickly. This is called deceleration.

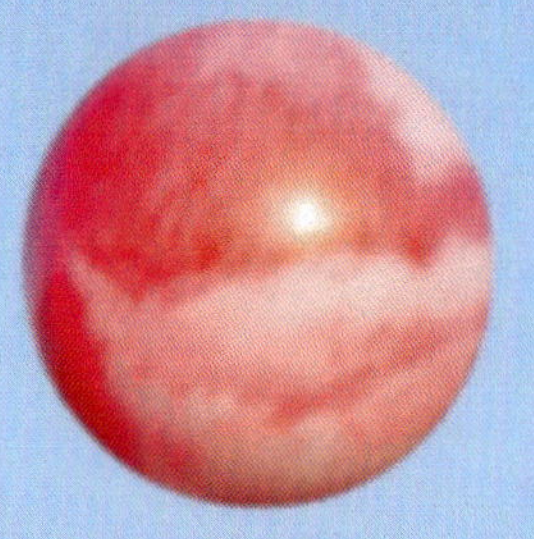

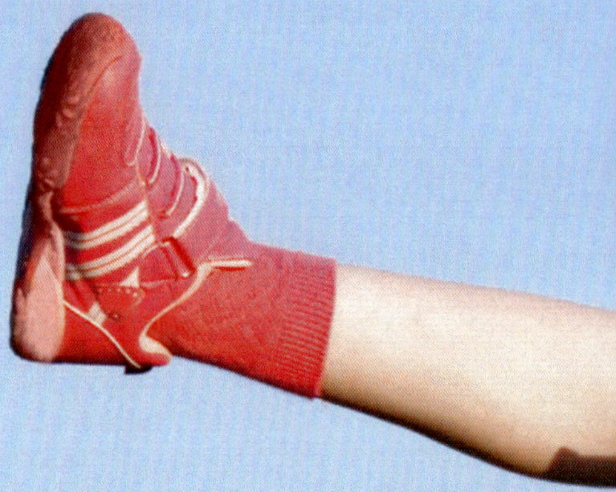

Changes in Motion

Inertia makes things resist changes in motion. Objects at rest won't move unless a force gets them going.

A kick from your foot makes the ball fly across the field. The kick is the force that moves the ball. Stepping on a bicycle pedal makes the bicycle move. Pushing a toy car makes it zoom across the room.

A rolling ball, a speeding car, and a falling raindrop will keep moving until something stops them. Inertia makes moving things keep on moving.

Inertia also keeps things moving in one direction. It takes an outside force to turn or spin something. Your bike won't turn unless you move the handlebars. A kite won't dip without wind.

When two objects touch or collide, they push on each other and can change motion.

Think of a baseball game. The pitcher throws the ball to the batter. The batter swings the bat and hits the ball. The collision with the bat changes the motion of the ball. It zips by in the opposite direction.

Facts About Friction

A ball you kicked rolls across the grass. As the grass rubs against it, the ball slows down and stops. This rubbing is called friction. Friction is a force that makes things slow down or stop moving.

Anything that rubs can cause friction—even air! People who design airplanes think a lot about how to keep air from slowing down a plane.

Different surfaces create different amounts of friction. Cement is rough. Ice is smooth. Cement produces more friction than ice.

You can skate on ice. You can also slip more easily on ice. The tires of a car roll along on cement. But they can spin around and around on ice.

Gravity

Your backpack slips off your shoulder. What is the force that got it going? When you throw a ball into the air, why does it fall back down?

Earth's gravity is the force that pulls everything down toward the ground. Anything that has mass has gravity. We can't see it or feel it, but we know it's there.

Flying Through Space!

The world is full of motion you can't sense. Right now, you are speeding through space! You are on Earth, and Earth is spinning around and circling the sun.

Even though it looks like the sun moves across the sky, it's not. Earth is moving. As the part of Earth you are on turns toward the sun, it becomes day. As the same part of Earth turns away, it becomes night.

Motion All Around

Leaves are fluttering. Raindrops are falling. Cars are whizzing by.

Look for motion and the forces that create it in everything around you. How many can you find?

Testing Friction

Without friction, it would be hard to stay in one spot! The amount of friction there is depends on the type of surface. Try this fun experiment to find out which types of surfaces create the most and least friction!

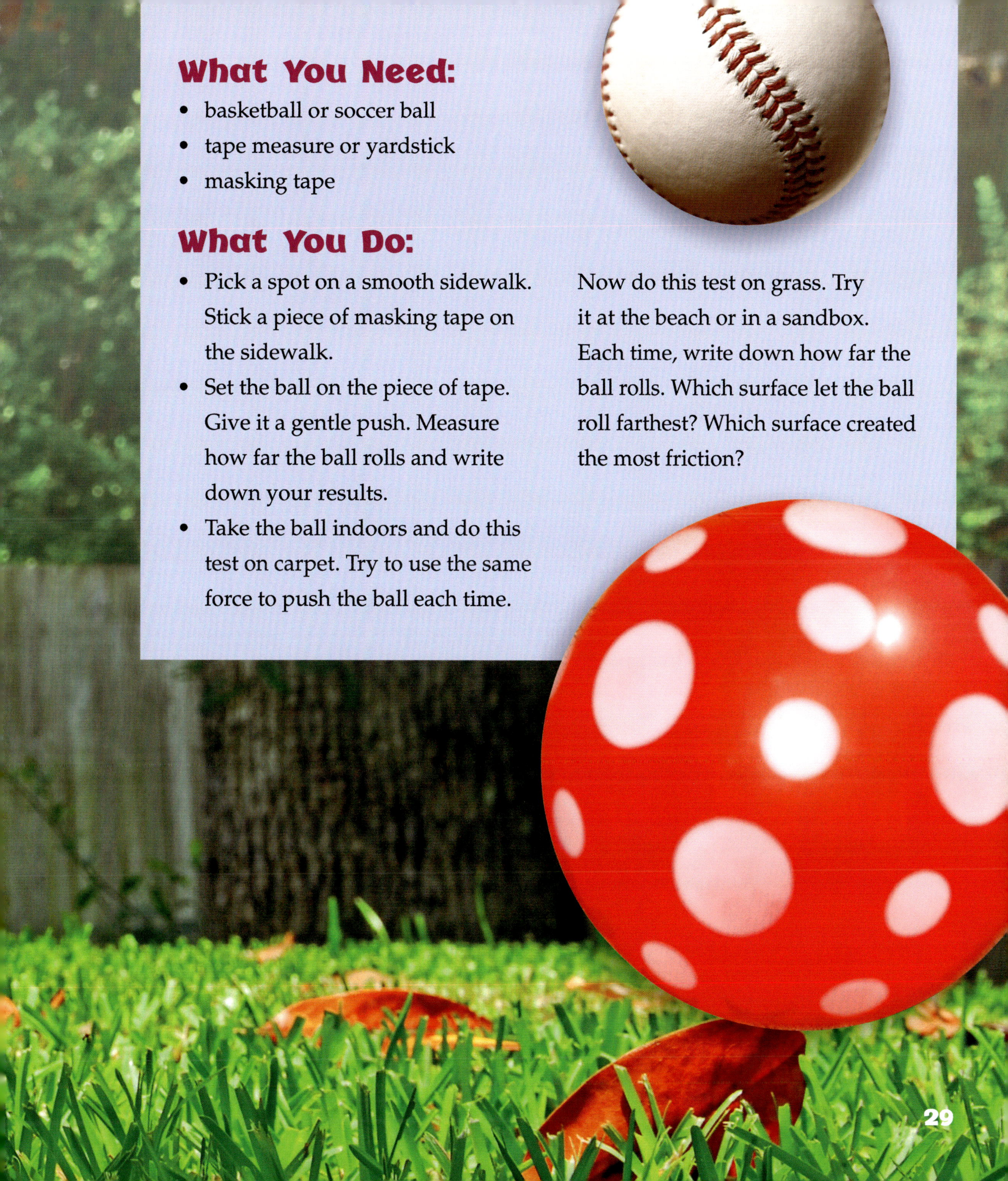

What You Need:

- basketball or soccer ball
- tape measure or yardstick
- masking tape

What You Do:

- Pick a spot on a smooth sidewalk. Stick a piece of masking tape on the sidewalk.
- Set the ball on the piece of tape. Give it a gentle push. Measure how far the ball rolls and write down your results.
- Take the ball indoors and do this test on carpet. Try to use the same force to push the ball each time.

Now do this test on grass. Try it at the beach or in a sandbox. Each time, write down how far the ball rolls. Which surface let the ball roll farthest? Which surface created the most friction?

GLOSSARY

acceleration—speeding up

collision—when two things run into each other

deceleration—slowing down

friction—a force produced when two objects rub against each other; friction slows down objects

gravity—a force that pulls objects together

inertia—a property of matter that makes things resist changes in motion

mass—the amount of material in an object

motion—movement

speed—how fast something is moving

READ MORE

Housel, Debra J. *Motion.* Physical Science. Huntington Beach, Calif.: Teacher Created Materials, 2015.

Hyde, Natalie. *What Is Motion?* Motion Close-Up. New York: Crabtree Publishing Company, 2014.

Troupe, Thomas Kingsley. *Are Bowling Balls Bullies?: Learning About Forces and Motion with the Garbage Gang.* The Garbage Gang's Super Science Questions. North Mankato, Minn.: Capstone Press, 2016.

INTERNET SITES

Use FactHound to find Internet sites related to this book.

Visit www.facthound.com

Just type in 9781543512274 and go.

Check out projects, games and lots more at **www.capstonekids.com**

CRITICAL THINKING QUESTIONS

1. Some things move quickly, like a baseball or a race car. What other things can you think of that move quickly?
2. Cement produces more friction than ice. What is friction? Hint: Use your glossary for help!
3. What is the force on Earth that pulls everything down toward the ground?

INDEX

acceleration, 11
airplanes, 4, 19
balls, 13, 17, 18, 22
cars, 4, 9, 13, 14, 21, 26
deceleration, 11
Earth, 24, 25
forces, 12, 13, 15, 18, 22, 23, 27
friction, 18, 19, 20
gravity, 23
inertia, 12, 14, 15
pulls, 10, 11, 23
pushes, 10, 13, 16
speed, 9, 11, 24